To Amelia,
I love you infinity x infinity +1

Inspired by my Mother
to live a life of adventure

Some Grandmas like to drink tea
and sit all day in the sun,
their hair is neat and tidy in a little tiny bun.

They like to knit a sweater while they rock in their chair,
and they pass the time of day away without a single care.

BUT not my Grandma!

She likes adventure and fun!

My Grandma has cooked on a campfire
and had to hide her food from bears.
Then, she strapped on her hiking boots
and climbed a thousand stairs.

When she finally reached the top
she sat and enjoyed the view.
The sun was shining, the clouds below,
and the sky was very blue.

My Grandma peddled her way across Europe
with Grandpa on a bike.
She made it all the way to Africa
and found a hill to hike.

The giraffe and the zebra just stood still and stared.
There goes one determined lady,
and they were kind of scared.

My Grandma has driven Hawaii in her bright orange van, and explored the deep blue waters on a sailing catamaran.

She spent her days snorkeling and spotting pretty fish;
a humu here, a honu there,
her fins went swish, swish, swish.

My Grandma travels the world by air or land or sea.
She walked the Great Wall of China,
then sat and drank green tea.

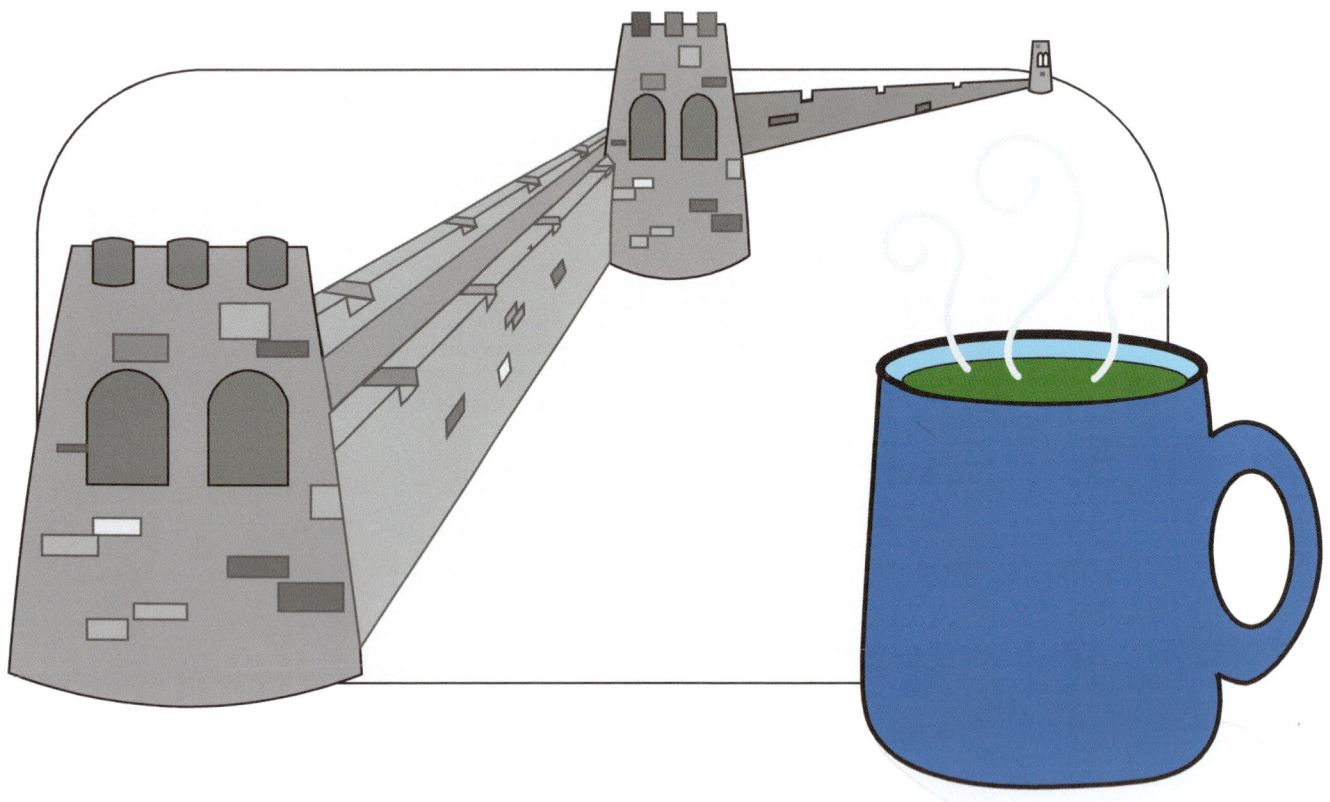

And when the snow began to fall
she headed for the hill,
a bumpy sleigh ride to the bottom,
but what a great big thrill.

My Grandma went to Australia
to see her first born son.
They flew all the way to Uluru just to have some fun.

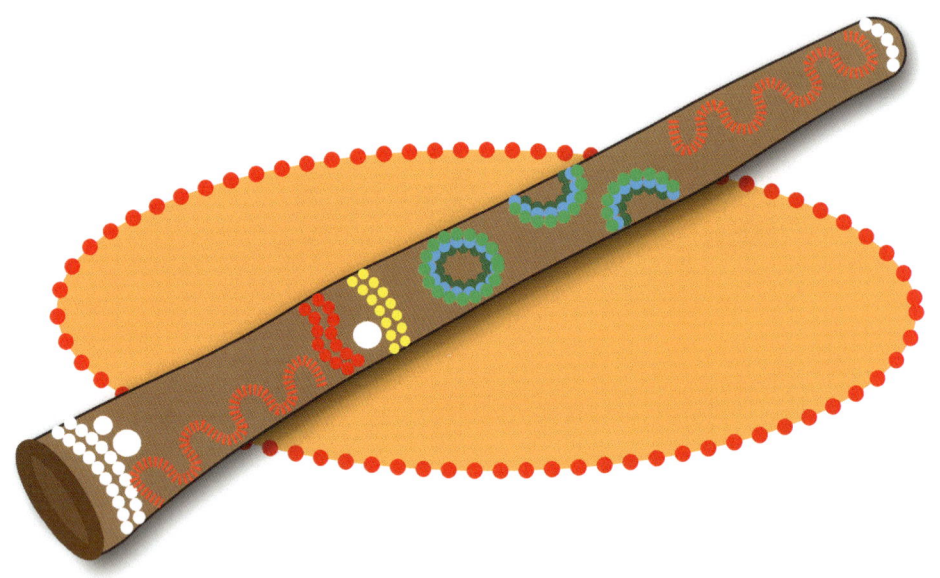

They learned about the local tribes
and played with kangaroos,
and when the day was all but done
they played the didgeridoos.

But, the best thing about my Grandma
is when she comes to stay.
She'll sit and tell me stories
and I'll play with her all day.

My Grandma will pretend with me
and we'll make the yard a mountain.
What about that big WATERFALL?
It's really just the fountain!

We'll make a cave from blankets,
and go searching for some bears.
Look for lurking lions underneath the stairs.

And, once we've gathered all the toys
we'll invite them for some cake.
We'll put on hats and fancy gloves
and hand out food we make.

Our ship has sunk into the sea, "Oh my, what a scare!"
Thank goodness I'm safe from sharks, on my little island chair!

My Grandma will come rescue me in her trusty little boat,
then we're back to our castle surrounded by a moat.

My Grandma says her favorite trips are those she has with me.
It doesn't matter where we are, or what we get to see.
As long as we're together, it's where she wants to be.

Hearts
By Amelia, Age 5